REVIEW

"A revealing look behind the curtain at the still-seamy world of televangelism, told by someone who was there."

— Darryl Johnson, author of "The Last Call"

"For those who believe Rev.Bakker has truly repented for his past transgressions..."

— Anthony Zolezzi, author of "The Detachment Paradox"

"From a harrowing childhood to his near-miss at stardom, the author weaves an amazing story of hope, agony, optimism."

— Rhonda Kayo Gibson, author of "Released"

AMERICA HAS TALENT/ AGAINST THE GRAIN

JOHN COLLINGS

AMERICA HAS TALENT/AGAINST THE GRAIN

iUniverse books may be ordered through booksellers or by contacting:

iUniverse
1663 Liberty Drive
Bloomington, IN 47403
www.iuniverse.com
844-349-9409

ISBN: 978-1-6632-1568-0 (sc)
ISBN: 978-1-6632-1570-3 (hc)
ISBN: 978-1-6632-1569-7 (e)

Print information available on the last page.

iUniverse rev. date: 12/22/2020

INTRODUCTION

Covid-19 is all over the nation right now, and no matter how much we wish we could ignore it, there's no way to prevent it from changing our daily lives. People are hella tired of being shut in. and of not making any money! Before this wet, massive load of shit hit the world's fan, I thought 2020 would be marked by my turning over a new leaf, and making my life profitable again. And maybe it will, because here I am writing my second book, the follow-up to **Tantalizing Quest.**

On the Today Show, they just told America that the virus will likely become worse in winter with the arrival of the kind of weather that so often brings on a bad flu! On the other hand, it didn't vanish or even diminish when summer weather came - except for people in countries with intelligent leadership that imposed stringent rules to limit the spread, followed by gradual, sensible re-opening strategies. In other words, people who don't live in Brazil or Russia or Russia's closely affiliated satellite the United States of America.

But here we are, watching the new cases and subsequent deaths climb, saddled with a baby-man president whose egg shell ego won't allow him to admit any of his thousands of mistakes are, in fact, mistakes. A president with the manner of a swaggering televangelist, preying on those in the populace who - possibly for lack of good schooling - have deficiencies in sort truth from fiction. Especially from fiction that stokes racism, homophobia, and fear of what tomorrow may bring.

The Trumpian mistakes that go unowned and unclaimed are grievous ones, as it turns out, and have made the Good Old USA number one in sad categories where you'd expect Third-World nations to be the top contenders.

In such an atmosphere. I have decided to compose a Dear Thomas John letter to my former employer, the resilient and resourceful Jim Bakker. Yup that's right, it's Mr Televangelist t to you!

THE NOT QUITE SO NEW JIM BAKKER SHOW

I was the one who put Jim Bakker into his black turtle neck shirt, dressing the poor man and performing little manscaping touches- *careful with the blush!* - For his first publicity photos to hype his "thrilling" launch of "The New Jim Bakker IV Show," which would also be the debut of his newest wifely "side kick," young(er) Mrs. Lori Graham Bakker!

They were both odd and, very predictably they comprise an odd couple. Their age difference was stunning, for starters. Nearly two decades. But he had previously been first in his field of television, the sub-genre of heavenly hucksterism called "separating fools from their cash with religious hogwash."

Lori, having not a clue how to do television but desperately wanting to succeed, was not yet burdened with the realization that she didn't have a prayer of ever reaching the potential of her predecessor, the tear-duct queen, the reigning duchess of mascara-melting, Tammy Faye Bakker. After all, Tammy (unlike the more conventionally brain-wired Lori, could cry at the drop of a dime! And her T-shirts old like hotcakes, featuring just two enormous eyes and dark pools of make-up running down, and the simple phrase: "I just

_____". It was a ridiculous level of stardom that Lori could never display the capacity or talent to achieve! Tugging the heartstrings of gullible people is a crass act that must be perfomled with n air. Tammy Faye had it. Lori hadn't figured out what it was.

Don't get me wrong. I loved Lori., he was sweet back then. I remember seeing her head off to her first Christian Woman·s breakfast! It was a debacle from which she returned crying. Not the crocodile, for-profit tears of her predecessor, but actual tears of humiliation and shame. She and couldn't figure out why the other women hated her so. (Informed sources think it may be traceable to the weasel whom she chose to marry.)

She might have looked at the headlines Jim Ba kker had genera ted, and might have rca li/cd she had po itioncd herself at the exact point where that paper trail would lead even Christian women. Jim Bakker had been indicted in 1988 on eight counts of mail fraud. 15 counts of wire fraud and one count of conspiracy. Sic transit one multimillion dollar televangelism empire. Now, that's something to cry about! Even though thirty-plus years have elapsed since PTL- the "Praise the Lord" club - had crumbled, Bakker reportedly still had unpaid IRS tax liens against him individually and also jointtly with Tammy, who died in 2007, totaling five-a nd-a-half million bucks.

Their combined abilities in fleeing the unwary had resulted in the building of Heritagc USA, a 2,300-acre Christian theme park and resort located in Fort Mill, South Carolina, a few miles south of Charlotte. In its top year, Heritage USA pulled in six million marks - excuse me, customers. They had a water park, which some said was just one other way in which they got soaked. Another was being allowed to pray in the Upper Room, which sorta looked like the selling for The Last Supper. The greatest thrill, though, was their opportunity to watch and cheer as Tammy Faye emoted for the cameras, and turned on the waterwork until it was time for Jim to repeatedly redirect audience attention to the donations box. Reportedly, some people were so moved by the spirit, instead of plain old cash they sent the Bakkers mink coats, diamond rings, and property deeds.

As tireless servant of God, Jim and Tamm y Faye found ways to divert enough donations toma ke people wonder if PTL was short for "Pass the Loot," including lovely vacation homes, opulently expensive cars to park around them, and the air-conditioner bolted to the roof of their dog's separate dwelling. Because that South Carolina humidity, you know.

This was the baggage Jim Bakker carried. (He's picked up pl enty more since.)

But Lori's only interest was in being "on TV," and how cool that was going to be. Surely, Jim could give her all the pointers he'd given Tammy Faye. Or perhaps all that Jim really wanted for her was to serve as his beard. The yang to his yin (but without reference to any cu lture from beyond these American shores), his good and infinitely supportive lady right by the side of a man dedicated to servicing Our Lord.

In plain terms, Lori was there to be his sex ua l cover-up.

What's that you ay? I low do I know this?

Jim Bakker had his goons try to coerce me to take a ride on the "casting couch." For which I said "no.'" And very soon after found that I was no longer employed on his television show! The same show that he was then trying to resurrect through the help of Jerry Craw ford, an exceedingly rich investor and a man who never minced words! Crawford's riches funded Bakker' move to Branson, Missouri, the Nashville of the Ozarks, as home base for the laughable "New Jim Bakker Show." There was of course, nothing really "new" about it beyond Lori subbing in for Tammy Faye. The "New Jim

Bakker Show" was the old dog, who seemed to have learned no new tricks in his pri son stay, which started in 1989 and involved a new name - Inmate 07407-058.

Bakker set his feet onto greased skids in 1980, when, according to a then 21-ycar-old "church secretary" later to become an actress, model, and frequent Howard Stem show guest, he and fellow preacher John Wesley Fletcher drugged and raped her. (By the way. psychiatrists say that when two men "share a conquest" simultaneously, they are in fact celebrating and cementing a homosexual bond, whether they rcalilc it or not.)

That 21-year-old was Jessica Hahn, of course. We all learned about her in 1987, when Bakker stepped down as head of PTL Satcllite Network and Heritage USA after his three-way with Hahn and Fletcher was made public. Hahn had reportedly gotten $279.000 to stay silent. Almost like a preview of the recent-times Donny Trump/Michael Cohen/ Stormy Daniels soap opera, in which the bagman went to prison and the guy who gave the orders is still commuting in Air Force One.

PTL funds bought I Lahn's cooperation, and Bakker was closely in charge of all of that organization's financial matters. A job so demanding that it required two sets of books. What would Jesus do? What else would Jesus do when reporters from The Charlotte Observer began writing about in vestiga tions into PTL finances.

I found out about Bran on. MO through a friend who thought it would be a great place to get recognition for my singing abilities. (I have a number of songs on YouTube.) Auditions were my way of life, and to it felt to hope that I might connect once again with a great opportunity!

Lately Jim Bakker has been in the news again, proclaiming a cure for the Covid-19 virus. That's laughable, yet sad when you think of all the people not only gelling fleeced but also possibly dooming their own health by believing a charlatan. But Jim will proclaim anything to make a buck.

Lori's mom "Char" is someone you'll always remember, once you meet her. She will remind you of that well-known black and white sketch which, if viewed from one direction, looks like a fairy princess - until you tum it up ide-down and rcali/c that it's a picture of the witch from "now White," waiting to ofler unsuspecting children an apple. Char offered me —oops, made me - sign a form stating that l was a "Born-Again Christian."

One of the main requirements was to sing and si ng well. But apparently you had to be in their cult to draw a paycheck. Which sounds an awful lot like illegal discrimination in hiring processes. Somehow, I don't think William Barr is likely to prioritize that investigation.

On a March 4lh broadcast this year, Jim opined "We are asking people to give an oflcring and we need a miracle. Your products are going to come to you. Every one of them will come right to your house and if we can't, we are going to refund. I will sell part of the buildings at Morningside." A very sizeablc amount of the New Jim Bakker Show was devoted to stoking people to fear for their survival, what with the Godless forces threatening to tum their (very white) world upside-down anytime in the future. Properly frightened, these people would then buy survivalist supplies, canned goods and the like, to ensure they'd make it through Annageddon, with plenty of snacks for thei r trip to G loryland on Tnat Old Gospel Train.

There was a woman who sold her two homes to benefit the Jim Bakker Organization, then went to live on the Jim Bakker Properties. Once the money ran out, they said all kinds of bizarre crap about her and tossed her out of his compound. If he cannot use you for some reason, either working for him for free or contributing to his cash flow out of your own pocket, you're gone!

When Char heard that I had makeup experience with a company called G lamour Shots, it was determined tha t I would augment my singing duties with making Lori look divinely pretty. Glamour Shots had been quite a big deal in the 80's and 90's. We would dress people up in costumes of their choice, from fantastic to just plain strange, out of a huge collection of costumes and accessories. I was trained to do their hair and make-up and guide them to, like Madonna says in her song, strike a pose! And even adjust their arms, tilt their head, get some seriously fun pose working, and then take lots of photos for God's sake. The customers would find plenty of something indefinably fantastic from all of the time and effort! But it was really more than that it was the experience, so it took a lot of pumping them up and getting them excited about this extremely fun time.

What the hell, there was nothing else around like this, and for their time in the spotlight each person became our one and only focus, as if there was no other person in the world. I made them feel that way, and was extremely great at it. That customer, once in my chair for their alloted half hour, found that their entire demeanor changed. They were no longer dull or everyday. They felt like a "celeb." That was what I was trained for, and I knew that this skill set could pull m e forwa rd in life and make me a better person.

Part of the Glamour Shpts experience was true. The other part was fantasy. They were just regular people. not "movie stars," but with creative makeup, coaching, and clothes that look the part, they felt like a successful product of the celebrity culture that we all find so endlessly intriguing. And in fact the photographs were often quite awesome, and the training made me more adept at being a salesman.

Which I suppose made me kind of like Jim Bakker, only with the difJerence that I gave people something to treasure and to share with family and friends. When Jim gets your money, you receive a dream. It's great for the moment, but in time you figure out you've gotten nothing in retum, a ll you can say is "Oops!" And you take that age-old vow: "Fool me once. shame on you. Fool me twice, shame on me.

Really, all televangelists are the same. They want beaucoup bucks and don't care about the people they're scamming, no doubt in my mind. Seeing it for the first time, and with my own eyes, was not pleasant.

I remember meeting during auditions the son of Kate Smith - who was known for her stalwart recording of "God Bless America"-and thinking he was surely going to get the singing job because of who his mother was. lie was a super nice guy, but unfortunately, a flaming and creaming queen —and I don't mean the grandmother of Harry or William! He couldn't fulfill the code as practiced by Bakker and many other hypocrites: Keep your urges under wraps, maintain great control, and you're in like Flynn. But if Jerry Crawford, the money bags of the operation, caught wind of overt gayness, you would get his size 13-wide boot in: sertcd a t speed right where the sun don't shine. Any Q?

Jim Bakker was well-versed and trained, and had figured out by reading the receipts that he had an awesome talent. If things were diifferent, and Tammy Faye Bakker would have waited for him while he did his "bit" in the penitentiary (insert here a chorus of "Stand By Your Man"), he might have gotten everything back and then some. In their primes, Jim and Tammy Faye were an unstoppable team.

Lori could never compare! But if she would have watched more old videos of Tammy Faye Bakker's performances, and thereby had learned to act, and thereby induced Jim stop calling her stupid, who knows how much loot they could've collected'

As my foster parents would always say, "Praise in public, and save the other stuff for behind closed doors."

This is something Jim had not been taught, or just didn't care to learn. I believe from personal experience that his ego is way bigger than you can imagine- which may be why it was so difficult getting his head through the turtleneck pullovers he favored.

Seeing Jim Bakker return to the airway probably broke Tammy Faye Bakker's heart, after all the various ups and downs of her post-PTI, existence. Whatever the reason, she went down quick. Just like Scripture says. "We are like ripples in the water."

I was constantly feeling bad for Lori. I knew for a fact that he would make her cry, telling her "you're not good enough."

Well, one good thing is that he will not have to wait long for him to kick the bucket. Although I believe she really loves him, the feelings are not reciprocated.

The last note I got back from Jim was devoted to expressing how much he missed me. This came after I got an attorney, an event that he knew all about. He basically wanted me to come back. Sorry, though, I'm not into three-ways that include certain dynamics.

PRINCE HARRY AND MEGHAN MARKLE

All through history, people have wanted to be them - the upper crust, the elite. Meghan Markle is no differcnt, and smashed some of her closest friends, such as the English gentleman Piers Morgan, who was one of the judges from America·s Got Talent, a competition for which I recently flew to Las Vegas.

You see "the Royals" have been more to me than they are to most people. My grandfather was with the Royal Mounted Police. His career status was blessed by the Queen. I just wish I had his uniform. You know, as something to put on display or leave in the cedar chest with mothballs: A legacy, proud to put in his line of descent, with my head held high and my chest puffed out! Mother was so proud of him and often said, "If only you could have met him. A good man to the bone."

Meghan Markle made it possible and awesome for little girls of all races to believe they could have the "FAIRY-TALE." Of course, and then get selfish and fuck up both families.

The truth be known, there is a lot you need to know about becoming a "royal." You don't just put on the pretty clothes and slap on a crown before getting served your eggs over easy with a breakfast cooked to perfection. And in her eyes, kneeling before the "Queen" was just dreadful. Who could ask you to do such a thing? Why it would make you feel like less of a person, and since we're from America, we are much better than that. We couldn't possibly bow before anyone. Why, people should kneel before us. Or so folks like Meghan believe.

Rules and regulations are not a part of Meghan's worldview. She is after all from LA, home of the only people in the world who count for anything. LA is filled with people of pride, as they make sure you know! But for God's sake, "I can still use the royal title, but not have to live and kneel before anyone..."

Watching this royal drama and trauma unfold is quite remarkable: It illustrates how selfish people can be, striving to acquire it all, no matter whom you step on to do it. In my eyes. Meghan Markle is ruthless. I recently heard that she is the voice in a documentary about elephant, out of the Disney organization. I'll never watch it, if only because of how she achieved her stature.

Barbra Streisand, one of the biggest and most accomplished entertainers of all times, met Prince Charles once. She shared her thoughts feelings over cups of tea. Who knows? If she would have been even nicer to him, she might literally have become the first actual Jewish-American Princess!

There have been a lot of commoners who have taken on the title of "Royal." But only the real prideful, those who are really into themselves, change their minds and opt out. It often turns out that the role was way more demanding than what they had thought, and beyond what they could handle.

Poor little Archie, for what that little guy will go through in the long run, particularly the not knowing what might have been in store for his and his family's future. One thing's for sure right now. They could have been protected more from the Covid-19 virus, living out on one of the royal estates, tucked away from the fear of this pandemic!

Princess Diana would have loved little Archie. I'm sure. His pictures are adorable, and at least his parents are sharing them with the public. That I find strange, because Meghan Markle has a thing about suing the tabloids. Well then, don't share anything. Keep your lives private and not public! So now we know the game plan: Sue the tabloids, get money.

The supermarket tabloids did stories about me a few times, concerning my connection with televangelist Jim Bakker, a well known television personality who loves money and will cry, scream, do anything to obtain that good ol' mighty dollar. I didn't scream and jump up and down, or cut myself for that buck. To me it was an honor, just to be selected as newsworthy, and a thrill to know that people actually bought copies just to read about us!

And what will Prince William do, except maybe a few speaking engagements? I'd go to catch one, and even spend $400 a plate for a dinner and reception featuring the young prince. Really, did Prince Harry have the slightest idea that this was all going to hit the fan, to use an American term? It was bound to fall apart, and fall apart it did.

If you're going to do it, "Go big or go home" as they say! Meghan Markle complains about people not liking her because of her being part black. Well, girlfriend, only in America can you claim the race card so easily. It's the going thing in America to try to pull off a bold move such as that. But the Brits think that it's all poppycock! And should be flushed down the loo (toilet). And for heaven's sake, not for one instant do I believe that the royals treated her any differently. I'm sure she perceived it the wrong way, and if something doesn't feel right it's a black thing. I'm just saying— I'm 25% Native American, but you don't hear me bitchin' about all the land that was taken, and our people made slaves as well. It's water under the bridge. Get over it! We've had a black President, so move the fuck on already! As Babs once said: "Bab's digs nails into Prince of Wales." It's for sure that Prince Harry loves his son. You can feel it in the photos he shares!

My daughter could have handled being a "royal." She's very outgoing. beautiful, and handles herself quite well in both her personal and public life. At this point I'm sure the Queen is oblivious to all that is going on with Meghan, and Prince Harry and misses the grandchild and Harry. How difficult it must be, not having them around and not being able to hold the grandchild, and I'm sure she wishes she was guiding Meghan on how to bring the child up with dignity and respect.

My hope is that Meghan and Prince Harry are thoughtful and visit the Queen often. She is getting older and one must keep that in mind, of family gatherings. No matter how we look at the flap within the royal family, the Queen deserves respect at all times. She needs to come first with all the major discussions that Prince Harry and Meghan Markle make while raising a royal child.

CRYSTAL 2 CARS

It's never easy meeting new people. There's always the instinctual drive to want to wow them. That's just a genetically coded aspect of who we are, our pack-animal natures.

That's how it was with this meeting. I had just moved to Las Vegas. My room-for-rent fell through. I was not handling it well, so suddenly my stress level was extremely high -as measured in the pounds I'd begun gaining at a steady rate. So that was what had me entertaining the thought that I could relieve my stress by sitting for some pleasant moments in a bar, maybe coming across an opportunity to meet someone, whereby I might by chance learn of a room for rent, and increase my odds of staying off the street.

I had previously talked with some homeless guys, and they were helpful. Some of them had found a bush to rest under to ride out the heat in Las Vegas. which in the summer could reach 120 degrees. Daytime shade was extremely important, just as much so as a supply of fluids, a must. The heat can eat your lunch in no time flat. It's merciless to all who walk in it, especially those with no place else to go!

People live there in the open - "wearing the pauper's crown" of the blue sky, as the English sometimes put it - because of jobs that were lost and of course, because of gambles that use their every last dime. Kind of like the guy who, in the old joke came to Las Vegas in a $30,000 Chevy and after one night at the tables he came home in a $250,000 Grey hound bus. Except these were the people without bus fare, or a home to go back to. Hell bent on survival and believing that the last dime is the "lucky" one, and that one last pull on the handle will make them millions. And you ask, how would I know this? Because of my experiences with a former roommate, and the two of us traveled to Las Vegas at one point, searching for a possible new chapter in our lives. When I met him he owned his own flower shop in Burlington, Iowa, where he and I could be frequently found on the riverboat."Catfishbend." That's when that boat was still on the river, and always packed. In Covid times, that boat is only a memory.

One woman we heard about did win $1 million on the penny machine. Okay, one person out of a zillion, and others thought they could, once the word got out! With my friend being a regular, casino workers knew us, and had a great respect, knowing he was going to spend chunks of money, usually at least $20 on each hand of blackjack or roll of the dice. We even moved to Las Vegas, but the floral business there was so much different, so we eventually moved to Dallas.

Anyway. there I was back in Las Vegas again. sitting in a bar, drowning my bad experiences and checking out the clientele. I wasn't feeling the best,. but I was determined that I would make the best out of a bad sitituation! It was on a Tuesday night, with not too bad of a crowd at the Badlands Saloon. Remember this is Lost Vegas, NV, where people from all over the world come to break into the worldclass gambling league, and play for the gold alongside all of those other big dreamers.

Years prior, my wife and I stopped in for a go at that dream, but that's for the next chapter. Talk about being a chunk, I must have been 2000 and something, not long after I figured out Badlands Saloon, wasn't just any kind of bar. It was a gay bar first and a western bar second, no matter what the name of the place would suggest. Anyway, "while in Rome..." as the saying goes!

I sat next to this guy and he spoke with kind of a stuck-up attitude, as if he was a high school teacher out to impress you with his storehouse of knowledge. After all, he was born and raised in Las Vegas, making him quite special and set apart from every other person who walked on Earth.

I, being in extreme dire need, thought "I need a room." I was desperate and, not desiring to live on the street. pushed the envelope and made advances. Very soon I found out that I was too large, and worst of all not a twink kid in his

20's. "Ted" (not his real name), bought me a few drinks and subsequently left with his much younger friends. Ted was much larger and older than I, and had some money to work with, in the form of an inheritance. Out he also had one sister, and somehow her name was on the titles of both houses their parents had left behind.

Moving right along, I then met a young guy, maybe twenty-nine, who was a guitarist and would play gigs in and around town. His favorite place in town was Fremont Street. It was a great environment for drinking: Five blocks packed with Las Vegas's old-town casinos, featuring numerous bars, live shows, and bizarre sighting like the guys in "G" strings, and the girls dressed as show girls, trying to make a buck by inducing you to take a picture with them. Some guys were street-smart, and dressed to look like babies in diapers to appeal to a certain clientele. Some were suited up as Chippendale guys, all impressive muscles lightly oiled to create a visually-arresting sheen. They would walk up to women and talk them into photos. You would also find panhandlers trying to get money for the next drink. I once met some people in Davenport, Iowa, who when I mentioned Fremont Street rolled their eyes like silent movie stars. They wanted me to know what they thought of the scene.

Being in a desert, when it did rain in Las Vegas it would pour and would not stop for hours, fast and furious the whole time. It would come down so hard, people told stories of how homeless men and women would stay in camps under the freeway overpass, and when they a big rain came would come they would get swept away or down. Convicts would also come to Las Vegas to run away and believe me, they would come in hard, so they say!

Anyway, I met this young guy that night at The Badlands, and he invited me to sleep on his floor. He was young, with blond hair and blue eyes. Very attractive, and a lot of older guys brought him drinks, hoping to get him drunk and take him home, and well, you know.

I took up his kind offer, followed by making breakfast when the next morning arrived, in honor of his being a cool dude who trusted me to share his pad rather than find a spot beneath an overpass. He advised me that from where we were, at Sahara and Las Vegas Blvd, I should proceed north until I reached 1501 North Las Vegas Boulevard. When I got there I would find a shelter called Catholic Charities. They had a full range of services, including providing a shelter that houses men. They allowed a person to have have one carry-on, just like the airlines. Not that I had a great deal of luggage to take care of. I was traveling light - just a trash bag stuffed with some clothes and a toothbrush, toothpaste, plus an underarm stick to take the worry out of being close. But I guess a lot of people travel light.

This young guy, not even knowing me, put me on his living room floor, and was nice not to smoke a bowl of his huge pot stash while I was there. The kitchen cabinets were filled with liquor, enough for me to be drunk and upchuck for a week. A lot of people in the industry drink or do drugs except the Osmond Family: More about them later!

He even gave me a duffle bag for my stuff, nice guy that he was. It packed more style than my straining Hefty Bag, for sure. I expected to be invited to join a better class of broke transients.

After I settled in at Catholic Charities, guys figured out I am well you know, receptive to the advances of others of my gender. Yet I felt totally safe there, even though I wasn't a big fan of being one of a pack of 15 guys taking a shower together: Always an awkward social event. I didn't care to say can you pass the soap! And even more careful to never let the soap squirt out of my hands. If something sexy and marvelous would have happened during my Catholic Charities stay, I would have definitely put it in the pages of this book. It's an autobiography and true story, and I'm holding nothing back!

After all the walking from place to place throughout Las Vegas in my attempts to get employed and generally back on my feet, I had been moving around on my feet long enough to shed quite a few pounds. One day I met two guys at the flower shop where I had begun working. They happened to go to the same church as Ted, the guy who'd left me in his dust at the Badlands Saloon. In the fulness of time. They re-introduced me to Ted. Me being in my trim new shape, he became interested. Even offered to take me places in his Mercedes, as soon as he got it out of the shop. Unfortunately, every time Ted got enough money together to ransom his luxurious Teutonic ride, he used his financial power to keep buying crystal meth instead! I'm sure that was fun for him, but it didn't improve his personality much. and that was what he needed most of all. Much more than he needed an air-conditioned luxury sedan.

VANCOUVER TEACH ME

I so wanted to meet my mother's side of the family! Like most families, they have fights. Nothing new, Ross and Adam are from the family of Tom, my mother's youngest brother, and his wife Barbra. Barbra was a very beautiful woman, with awesome skin, jet-black hair, and the coolest dimples on her charming face.

The only time Tom ever felt helpless was when Barbra contracted cancer. He absolutely fell apart, not knowing how to handle it. I am not sure I could handle being in love and then finding out that the person I loved had contracted an incurable ailment.

Her family was disappointed in him, but I sided with Tom. Not simply because he was my uncle, but because he was going through so much. I only saw Tom once after Darbra's diagnosis, and he looked in disarray, out of it. Not long after, he was found dead in a hotel located not far from where his brother, my uncle Paul, lived.

Paul was my mother's next-to-the-oldest brother. The family line-up goes like this: Ted Jr., Paul, Mom, and Tom, whom they called him Tommy.

My grandfather, their father, was a Pentecostal preacher who later in life turned into a missionary! So as kids and as grown-ups always got religion crammed down their throats, as well as into their thoughts. Later in life, they all rejected religion totally. Had absolutely nothing to do with it. You've heard the spiel: "Narrow is the path, and few find it!" And really, will any of us find it? Who knows? All we can do is search, and be open to whatever revelations, inspirations, enlightenment or positive vision we may be lucky enough to encounter in our lives.

In reality, most humans only look at these possibilities when they are on their death beds, poised to enter into another realm about which they have scarcely thought or dreamt of. Some simply do not care one way or another about what lie beyond Earthly experience. But I do believe in the notion that there is a bigger and more lasting reality, or perhaps a multitude of posibilities for experiences, beyond this life. And even that it is possible to find your way to knowing something about it, to at least some extent, perhaps·with a lot of study, if that is the direction you choose. I am all for someone who is in deep search. A lot of the search is just trying to find what works for you. Many years ago I was at that point, reaching and choosing, and that search was the inspiration when I recorded "'The Prayer," which you can see and hear on Youtube.com. Just type in The Prayer John Collings.

There is a driving force in the universe, whatever we may name it and however we try to define it. Some days it is extremely strong, and can feel it very powerfully. And I admit a sacred presence is there, and I try and reach out that driving force by praying every day.

My partner is not so much oriented to seeking out answers in this way. I can feel that he had been hurt, perhaps by people whose religious practices are tainted by a need to judge and even condemn others, and so I try to accommodate his attitude, and to feel what is going on in him. Certain things, I sense, are strong currents within his being. And I always try to remember that he had someone before me. Who know how that went? In one manner or another, it was a mix of good times and/or bad times, and obviously the bad times came to overshadow the good. Out that suffering is what made him available to connect with me. and I remain grateful that things turned out in a way that brought us together.

I knew his partner before. We hung out in the same circle, a very small circle.

Anyway, I would reach out to my cousins and try to get a feel for our family connection. I even did a Facetime chat with Ross, and it was a good time, just for that small time we chatted. I was really glad to be able to see who he looked the most like, his dad or mom.

That's always been a big thing in any family! Does he have his dad's eyes, his mother's hair?

How this all began was, I was on line with a guy and he said: "Yes, you can come stay here. My other roommate (meaning partner) is in another state, on business, (meaning in jail) for things he shouldn't have been doing."

Selling drugs, I'd imagine. It sounds easy enough, and I hear you can make chunks of money. But there can be the kind of repercussions that really suck, involving inmate i.d., jobs in the license plate fabrication business, and opportunities for group showers. I'm pretty sure that the outside of any given penitentiary is much more conducive to a healthy lifestyle than the inside.

Troy - my new roommate - kept this jailtime secret until I arrived. He wondered how I would take the news. Even though I am a former corrections officer, I believe I am still human. People occasionally do wrong things for some reason or another, maybe at times for a reason that sounded perfectly praiseworthy in the moment, as if it was the best resolution to some tough or highly pressured situation. one of us is perfect and life actually is, like a box of chocolates, Forrest: You never know what you're going to get until you commit to taking a bite.

There was a time, when I longer was a corrections officer, when I had done something that was not so smart. It related to the sexual abuse I'd experienced as a child, when I was nine and the guy who used me for his power-obssessed pleasure, forcing me to do oral, was 24. That incident changed my orientation at a crucial moment in my psychsexual development. After that incident I changed to wanting men. No matter how I would fight the urge, I couldn't. It was so strong.

Later in life when had gotten past my eighteenth birthday, I would frequently visit adult book store and compulcively watch porn. You can easily imagine the rest. Once I was hanging around and browsing in an adult bookstore at 4:30 in the evening. I had no idea that undercover cops were among the customers, pulling off a sting operation. One thing led to another, and this nice 40-ish officer with a pink polo shirt wanted me to follow him out to his car, after we'd eye contact as he observed me enjoying the coin-operated movie a little too much! But first I would go to the rooms in the theater and see the happenings, onscreen and around!

As hard as it was to break the cycle, the more I was drawn in. Drugs are strong, but things of the flesh are stronger, and fighting against sexual impulses can be almost too hard to handle. Our bodies can be so compelling, and sating our lusts and urges can at times be the predominant thought pattern, as if intelligence in many other parts of our bodies takes the leadership role briefly away from our conscious minds. Life has always been a struggle, and the systems implanted in our beings to impel us toward sex and reproduction have needed to be powerful for humanity to have gotten so far across the cons of evolution.

After getting to Vancouver, Washington, settling in was no problem. Troy and I found out that we had so much fun doing things together. We had similar interests, including watching old movies, and taking the bus to Portland, Oregon, only minutes away to experience a different city with different vibe. And of course party stores - or, as one of my friends say to his mom. "We met at the flower shop!"

But mostly, Troy would invite different guys over for party and play. That usually meant drugs and other things with which I was unfamiliar. I simply had never been down that road. I was so naive. "What's this called? A bong? Do you use it as a planter, or what?"

Troy was more than happy to show me how it all worked, from drug paraphernalia to drugfueled sexual get-togethers. Watching him with the other guys was an education in itself. We were not prostitutes, we never asked for money, but the guys Troy knew would bring crack cocaine and Tina (the local nickname for a certain drug), put it in the pipe for everyone to smoke it. It would always heighten my sexual drive. and guys would always leave happy. We were so good at hosting parties that before long we became very popular.

On the sexually-oriented phone lines, guys would line up and want to come over ASAP, and become a part of what we had. We actually became sexual fantasies for some, and to me it began to feel a little too dangerous. But Troy kept them coming and I had to admit that it worked for me. Our party scene became a fine, well-greased machine.

Playtime was something I did not want to give up, but ultimately my fear of getting caught was much stronger than the pleasures of the moment! "There was no way I was going to ruin my looks or let my teeth fall out from extended drug abuse. I remember that in high school we would sometimes get a lecture, either from a well-meaning teacher or from someone who was trying to pull their life back together after staying way too long on the drug scene. They would show us pictures of guys laying on the floor, knocked out, with pus streaming out of their noses, along with seepage of grease and other stuff out of noses and mouths.

I was so vain back then, if I thought something was going to age me, ending it was not at all difficult. But of course my withdrawal from the intense partying meant I no longer had that source of connection to Troy. The basis of our relationship shifted. I no longer seemed to be as much fun, I suppose, and my (relative) sobriety might have seemed to him to turn me into a sold or a reformer, or at the very least standing in judgement of the very activities through which we had bonded.

Besides, my goal of meeting more of my family was not going to happen.

My friend Bucky Heard, a singer with whom I often did duct, suddenly got a cool and impressive money-making gig. Bobby Hatfield, the higher-voiced singer of the original Righteous Brothers, had passed away. There was an opening for someone who could sing those parts.

The Righteous Brothers started out in 1962, when two guys from a larger vocal group decided to work as a duo. Troy's high range and Bill Medley's deep baritone meshed beautifully as they sang what would I utter be called "blue-eyed soul," and both guys were strong enough to take a lead voice for a whole song, or for a dramatic interlude. They were famous for presenting emotionally compelling performances, and had a bunch of hits in the 60s and into the 70s. When baby boomers got older, demand for The Righteous Brothers returned, and the duo was very popular again.

I got a job at a local restaurant, and saved money. It was time for Troy and I to part our ways, cut the ties and call it a day! After saying goodbye to him, which was very hard to do, I became very good friends with Bucky and we hung out a lot.

As much as I cared for Troy, I felt tha t tug to move on. Las Vegas, here I come! Taking a bus to the airport was like the saying goes "I took me a bus, and a train, and even a plane." But it's what it took just to get here!

You know when it's time to move forward, you receive it as a feeling you get in the pit of your stomach, and the faster you can yield to it, the sooner you will be on to another amazing adventure. But, of course, an adventure is by definition a situation in which you can not know what ultimately will happen.

BEYOND THE CLOUD — MOM

I remember the pain that I knew so well as a child.

We lived then at 20th Ave East in Moline, Ohio, a town situated where the Missisippi River get more immense by being joined by a sizable tributary which the Indians called Sinnissippi, but we call the Rock River.

Mr. Green, my father, the man at the center of my mother's life, was a good man who passed away much too soon! At one point I remember my grandmother saying how much he, Mr. Green, had loved my mom. But most people never survive a heart attack. and when it's time, it's time!

More husbands would follow. Rusty Osborn was the next lucky winner. Joyce was his offspring.

Rusty worked the rodeos and had a bullwhip. From what I was told, he on atleast one occasion used on my oldest brother, Chuck, or CB as he was called. Rusty loved the women, and while still married, he had a girlfriend.

At some point it became obvious to my mother that her relationship with this strikingly handsome man was coming to an end. My mother was quite a good-looking woman in her own right. Not Liz-Taylor-awesome, but certainly beautiful enough to attract handsome men. And she did. Usually someone, a friend, would introduce them. But for some reason, and I will never be sure what it was, mom would attract handsome men, but they were jerks.

Me and my brothers Harvey and Billy, and our sister Linda, were outside playing one day. All of a sudden, a Studebaker pulled up. A woman was driving and Rusty was in the passenger seat.

The car came to a fast stop, with gravel flying. Rusty jumped out of the car, left his door hanging open, and ran to the house. We heard loud yelling.

Suddenly, Rusty came running out holding little Joyce in his arm. My mother was not far behind. She kept screaming "Don't take her," and "Where are you going?" He jumped into the Studebaker, slammed the door, handed Joyce to his girlfriend, and with a child in her arms she proceeded to drive off. My mother clutched the doorhandle. The girlfriend sped up, pulling my mother half a block in the gravel. She tried her best to keep up, but as the car picked up more speed that made it impossible for her to stand on her feet and her legs were dragging in the gravel at the end of the half block, until her tired hands couldn't hold on any longer. Rusty won that battle.

As my mom laid crying on the ground, her legs bleeding, my brother Harvey helped her to gain her composure - not an easy thing to do after a driving car forces you to succumb to having your infant yanked away! What a thing that was for us small kids to see first-hand! Wow.

Most children will never experience such bad and fearful sights in their lifetime. They are blessed, just as all children should be. Children truly are new arrivals from heaven and should be consistently treated as such.

Bob, another man in our mother's life, was a guy none of us cared about. He was a con artist, and a womanizer. I'm sure any woman would find him attractive if she were blind. Whatever it was that made him seem attractive was somcthinbg imperceptible to our eyes. I thought he was boring and he had no class whatsoever. He definitely was not the usual kind of person my mother would choose! Not like my brother Patrick's dad, Herb, a tall, handsome guy born of Cherokee blood line! To be honest, Pat's dad and I tolerated each other but that was all. We had nothing in common, nor did we search through our backgrounds to investigate the possibilit y that we might somehow connect!

My father was of the Passamaquoddy tribe, a fact I never knew until much later in life. He was married to a woman named Jackie France, but clearly, they were having trouble on the home front. It probably wasn't her fault. She was awesome. It was clearly my a-hole father. He was a jerk, and that is an understatement. Every single thing was his way or the highway. and "his way" meant that if he wasn't the center of attention, we weren't going to do it. Jackie cooked, cleaned, got his meals, and he still wasn't happy.

My Jewish uncle Melton adored my mother, and mom was his first choice, he said something about it in 1994. He said that if my dad wasn't dating her, he would have married her!

Clearly our home life would have been better, and not the f-d up big mess that I was. I would have clearly been a nice Jewish Boy. But Melton made me promise never to say anything about his feelings for my mother. As the book says, the heart is a lonely hunter.

At my dad's funeral and wake, and the food prep afterwards, Melton had everything under control. I remember he wore his Air Force Fly boy jacket. You'd be surprised how much I think about him and my Native American-Jewish cousins. I'm sure I will never see my cousin again, since my dad's mother passed away one month after he did. You see, dad was grandmother's favorite, and he could not do wrong.

Although he did do wrong, and plenty of it, but she was blind to that fact.

My mother met my dad at the front door of his mom and dad's place. She was soon in love, and would have followed him to the ends of the Earth. My father was good-looking as it gets, and had the most beautiful singing voice. He would exercise it by singing on the radio, live. Some people thought he looked like Hank Williams Sr., and he would get mistaken for the Father of Country Music a lot in life. Until Elvis came along, Hank was a dominating presence and did a lot to bring country music into the mainstream. Even jazz crooner Tony Bennet paid attention to Hank Williams, cutting a version of Hank's hit "Cold, Cold Heart." You can see very old footage of him doing that song on YouTube.

My mother loved my dad's voice, but had no intention for him to share it with the world. Or maybe she had no intention to share him with the world, as if keeping him out of the spotlight would keep him faithful. She'd be upset all the time after he had done a radio show! A lot of females would ask him where he would hang out, if they might meet him sometime at a bar in town. They always wanted to meet him for a few drinks. and of course he was all for it.

Outside of racing his horses, chasing women was preferred his course of action. And my mother knew it. Once when she caught him in a bar talking to a woman, she grabbed a beer bottle off the bar and hit the woman in the head, knocking her off the barstool. My mother back then had a strong Irish temper, and used it well. One of the things my dad asked me in a conversation years l ater was "Does Dorothy still throw ashtrays?"

I told him "No. You no longer are a part of her troubles."

Their lives together had been rocky from the beginning. My grandfather particularly did not like my dad because of his being a man of color! The Irish had faced plenty of discrimination from the time they started arriving in America and remaking their lives after fleeing the great Potato Famine. They started at the bottom, even though they were no less white than all the people of English and other northern

49

European lines of descent, and they were willing to claw their ways up and out of permanent underclass status, just as Italian-American immigrants became desperate to do in their turn.

Meanwhile, my dad's mother was not really happy about mom because of her being white. So, there you have it, a marriage doomed from the start! Some things, and some loves, are never meant to be. Although at the beginning of any love relationship we want all of it to happen and to be as awesome as our imagina tions can picture! And so we give it our all, and try for the white picket fence, adorable dog. and the happy ending!

In 2019, mom passed, I had just graduated from MGM Culinary Academy in Las Vegas, only three days before my brother called from Texas to tell me the heartbreaking news.

Chuck, aka CB, had the closest relationship with her. Because circumstances required my being in foster homes, I didn't have as strong a cluster of memories to remind me what she looked like and what perfume she would always have on. A lot of what had been immediate reality gradually became just vague memories and distant thoughts. For her, I would just do the right thing, visiting her every other day when I lived in town. Our connection was really nothing to speak of, but I wanted it to be strong and I would try dearly to find a glimpse of whether she really cared or was I the one who had his heart on his sleeve. For whatever reason, I would visit all the time but my sister would hardly how. Meanwhile, Harvey's health was not that good, and with no car he had to rely on the bus, or else call me to get a ride. It was sad to hear about her exit, but all of us will go at some point. Her time came, so many of her best years wasted by men who weren't worthy of her, and there was no way to recapture the loss.

2ND STAR TO THE LEFT "AGT"

"America's Got Talent" Television show! Who knew how much times would change after that program came along? I remember the televisions show, "Star Search," which made stars out of people like Sam Harris, singer of "Over the Rainbow," and of stand-up comics such as Rosie O'Donnell and unknown or barely-known singers like Linda Eder!

By the time I was in 4th grade I knew I could sing well, and I would do it every recess on the playground, always drawing a crowd. It's impossible to express how much good that did for my young little heart. It was an audience of my peers, yet this God-given ability set me apart at the same time it joined me with them. I think we are all born artists, but the processing we get to make us fit into the world some how, to make a kind of commodity of ourselves that can be plugged into a job somehow someday, causes us to lose sight of how fulfilling it can be to exercise our creative muscles. In Balinese culture, practically everyone devotes time to expressing their artistic qualities. The refer to it as "Bringing the gods down to Earth." I was lucky enough to find out what I loved, and could excel in, and to win so much encoragemcnt, almost as a natural part of just growing up. I'll aJways be tlumkful for that.

One of the foster homes we kids lived in - that being me, my sister Lynn and brother Harvey was with the Thompson family. The Thompsons let me join The Moline Boys' Choir. This was a formative experience, for sure.

Kermit Wells, a frail individual and kind of a jerk, was the conductor. He had taken over after Dr. Swanson, an awesome guy whom the community had respect for and his students, including me, adored. Dr. Swanson was truly an extraordinary person, and he will always be deeply missed!

Life with the THompsons was extremely hard, though. We couldn't stay ovemight at a friend's house, and we were permitted no sports. They were afraid the dark secrets of the Thompson family would I ill their awful heads! These unspoken secrets included me being subjected to Roger Thompson's sexual desire, and our exposure to all the dancers who would come over a nd audition their routinefor the Thompson's stript ease bar! You can read the rest in my first book, **Tantalizing Quest 04240**.

It's quite a story how we escaped from the Thompsons at such a young age!

After my own divorce from Joy. I raised the kids with my then-partner Gordon Muller, a math teacher from Pleasant Valley Junior High in Le Clair, Iowa. Gordon was a good man, but he looked like a biker with his beard and long hair. His parents spoke Low German, or Plattdeustch, Gordon's grandparents came to America after the ordeal with Hitler. Germans were not really welcome here in America at that time, so they sruck to their own little communities throughout the

United States of America. After the kids were grown, Gordon and I went our separate ways. He wanted someone you nger, and I moved out!

I had by then met someone in Burlington, Iowa, when he visited the church I went to in Davenport, Iowa. He was a blend of Swedish and German stock, and he owned a flower shop in Burlington, a long the beautiful Mississippi River. He taught me how to make holiday wreaths and tabletop holiday trees with lights. I got really good at it/ He sold his house and a building that later became a deer hunting lodge with lots of land around it. He promised the money from the lodge sale to me. But I never saw a dime of it. That was just one of the many promises he never kept.

We did move together to Dallas. He had heard bout a church that he became gung-ho about, and we moved. All I knew about Dallas was that President John F. Kennedy's life abruptly ended there, and also that there was a television show called Dallas! However, it wasn't long before that relationship came to an end, He fell for someone else and I moved on.

Not long after, I met Larry - a stocky and loving, caring guy who had been in a great relationship up until the day his partner announced that he wanted someone younger. When Larry related this, I just said "Don't they all?"

Joan Rivers once joked that gays should be allowed to get married and be miserable like the rest of everyone!

Anyway, Larry's mom and dad were awesome. His father was the kind of man I wish I'd had as a father. And his mother loved her son and only child, just as much as he loved his parents, which was plenty.

Larry's dad and I soon became very good friends. He was very accepting, while his mother had her guard up. She knew that Larry's last relationship had ended up with his partner wanting to move on, going so far as to start a fight and even clock Larry in the head with a frying pan!

Larry put up with it for so long, and then moved out. So his mother, knowing that, wasn't about to let me waltz in without a thorough vetting. And it turned out that I would leave and come back, until eventually I left and never rctumed. Larry and I still call each other every other day! He eventually met someone awesome. We checked in with each other at a time when I went to Iowa to see my mother. By then her health was rapidly failing and there were days of her not knowing me. What could I do? I re introduced myself, and prayed for her mind to clear again - which it would, for a while.

Branson was the expanding entertainment capitol of the Show Me State, and I was going to let them show me something. This was my second adventure there, the first being with the Jim Bakker Television Show! And on my second time I met Angelina Woodhall, a writer of music. Music is her life and she was fabulous at it. Very creative and it was an honor for me to work with talent such as hers! She would do children shows with a big screen behind us of cartoons that she would create. Our shows were amazing and her ex-hubby, an awesome drummer, became a good actor as well. Which isn't hard to understand when you realize that both art forms rely on impeccable timing. Johnny Carson, the undisputed king of late-night TV hosts. was also a former drummer.

I got into booking our shows. One day, without notice, she decided to go to China and record a project she was working on. Before I knew anything, she was on a plane, from which she used an inflight phone to reveal the fact that these previously unheard-of plans were underway.

My response, "Wha t were you thinking of? We have show lined up!"

Obviously, I had to cancel our shows, and the people who managed the venues were not happy. I was much more than unhappy. I was furious and left Gainesville, Florida!

EARLIER DIALOGUE MADE IT SEEM LIKE WAS HAPPENING IN BRANSON.

While back in Iowa visiting mom, I began thinking about what to do. Branson in 2014, made me want to return. And so I did! While at work one day. riding in an elevator going down. I felt the car come to a stop and we waited while more customers came in the rough the sliding stainless steel doors. Right afier someone said, "Oh, going down?" someone else, out of the blue asked me "Do you want to come to my show?" It was a man with white hair and beard, speaking in a voice with a very soothing quality balanced with a note that revealed he was more than a little bit "determined. And what is your name sir?'" he inquired. "My name is Merrill Osmond."

You've heard of him. though the details may have slipped your mind. Merrill Osmond has performed all over the world in many prestigious settings. Before there was a Donny and Marie Osmond Show on television (for which Merrill served as executive producer), there was a quartet named The Osmond Brothers and a quintet called The Osmonds. Merrill was the brother who produced and wrote the music and lyrics for five Number One hit records. Merrill's smooth, confident voice you anchors such hits as "One Bad Apple," "Let Me In," and "Love Me for a Reason."

The Osmonds sang before the Queen of England and other prominent dignitaries. and appeared on the long-running' The Andy William Television Show.

I was one of those people just drawn to the talent as well as the look of Donny and Marie Osmond. Those smiles became a trademark, along with their voices and talent.

I found that talking with an Osmond was much easier than I would have thought. As Mormons. their faith is everything to them, and they always feel blessed to even have their careers!

Viril Osmond, one of the oldest brothers, is clinically deaf but nevertheless has a fine voice. He wanted to produce an album. I agreed to be at three shows. Going to the second one, I brought along a music CD of mine to give to Merrill. I was positive that he would never listen, and soon to sit in the trash. I was WRONG. He not only listened to it, he also played it for Jay Osmond. The next time I came in, Jay said "Here comes the singer!"

At the time I was working on new music and designing the CD jacket. So I proudly had Jay Osmond's phrase printed on the back.

Did the excitement end there? No! I was subsequently invited to go to a church in Hollister, Missouri, close to Branson. I met this guy from Alabama, a singer of Rock and Gospel, a man with long hair, who'd heard that I was a singer on The Jim Bakker Television Show, and The Kevin Shorey Television show. I opened Kevin's show, the very first singer! Kevin is the son-in-law of legendary Mel Tillis, and I became Mel's grandson's friend. That was Bucky Heard. whom I mentioned a couple of chapters back.

Bucky asked if we could duct together, and I said "Yes, that would be fun!'" And so we did and the crowd liked us. The band backing us up was Tony Orlando's, from the television show Tony Orlando and Dawn.

As mentioned before, Bucky Heard went to an audition with Bill Medley, who was looking to extend his career by hiring a singer who would be up for the challenge of re-creating the original recordings. Defending Bucky was difficult, but I felt I should. ever again will I do that. You've hear the stories about how some people change after they attain fame. If you are getting my implication, and wondering where I am going with this? I thought this could never happen, but Bucky Heard became a "born again Christian" for God's sake!

CHANCES ARE, RIVER WOOD

The lives we lead, for the most of the time derive from some aspect of our childhood which both leads us and drives us!

Things are never what they seem, but we deal with those issues at hand. We hope for the best, and try to overcome those obstacle. At times we think, "Is it even possible?" We wish we had a different life; it always seems that the grass is greener on the other side. A lot of time these thoughts are like playing at the casino: You spin the wheel, and when you win, awesome. But after you spin. do you lose?

When I was in Las Vegas, while being homeless I met a guy that was a doctor, a surgeon. His income was awesorne and he had a career that he hould have retired from with a good nest egg. He had moved to Las Vegas from Seattle, had a beautiful wife, and inhabited the kind of life a lot of people want and can onl y dream about. The problem is, they play the casino in other cities and towns too. Yes, you've won and your lucky streak keeps running well, and you've made chunks of money! Things look good and you feel unstoppable and conqueror of all things, cause the money keeps coming in and over fist!

But here's a news flash. Las Vegas was built on making money from people willing to take chances. Yes, some people walk away with money, and the casinos make sure to post those big winnings! Don't get me wrong, Las Vegas is fun and there are a lot of things to do besides gamble. You can ride the three-wheeler motorcycles, and find awesome places to shop, places for horse-back riding, hiking. the zoo, and impressive restaurants.

I worked at the Stratosphere, which kind of looks like the Space Needle in Seattle. Not only a casino, but rides too. And before people went to the top, yes, it's photo time. That was the most fun I ever had on a job, besides Glamour Shots.

Glamour Shots was a place where you could come in, get your hair and make-up done with professional flair, and get dressed up in the clothes that complete the picture. My first time working for Glamour shots was in Dallas, at a very large shopping mall, the Redwing Mall. What a great place that was, and we were alway busy. This company, just out of the gate, and their advertisers, did an awesome job because people were flocking to the Redwing Mall by the thousands.

Don't get me wrong, Las Vegas is a fun town. And North La Vegas is an education in itself. You see the homeless there in overwhelming numbers. As in most big cities it's almost becoming an epidemic, with destitute people everywhere.

I've heard the stories that some of the homeless enjoy being homeless, that some of them get a check, disability and food stamps, and don't want to live in a house. They have been homeless for so long that they are used to it. They don't have bills to pay and don't have to account for anything, and answer to no person! Myself, I never got that advanced into the homeless lifestyle. I scuffied until I found a way to work myself upward from that state. So I'm not a person who can identify with a desire for homelessness.

Weather in the Las Vegas summer is extremely hot - sometimes 120 degrees or more!! But remember, winter is also rainy season. and believe you me, the downpours are huge and there's flooding because of the sand, so usually water floods the streets.

Summer. if you walk, you always need to have plenty of water on hand. And when you're walking close to casinos, be very careful when crossing the streets. The drivers are from all over the world. No, really, they have some interestting ideas about who has the right-of-way, and whether or not pedestrians in their path are fair game! The cultural differences extend to maother facets as well, from dress and cuisine to how to act in a crowd.

You could be on a bus, in a casino, restaurant, bowling alley, sports arena, airport transit vehicle, etc., and the couple next to you are speaking a language you've never heard before, possibly from from a country you know nothing about. Which just makes Las Vegas all the more interesting, so many different kinds of people you see, or meet. Most of the time, the people visiting America do speak English, which probably is what gave them the confidence to come here and explore our country's major playground resort.

A lot of the speech is the English of England, rather than that of the USA. Quite a lot, of the people speaking with British accents, I found out, thoroughly hate President Donald Trump. When I was a photographer, they would state those views very assertively, as such much and want you to know and feel the force behind their feelings as they express their views.

Sometimes I feel that everyone should experience a span of months or years in Las Vegas, getting a job and plugging into one or more of the diverse aspects of local life. For me it has been a life-altering experience, a first-hand adventure that simply could not have happened in any other city in the nation or in the world.

--

Growing up the way that I did could not help but have a profound and lasting impact on how I see the world, and how I got conditioned via experience to respond to the people and situations I encounter in show business, and all the other aspects of my social existence, from lovers to casual acquaintances. Spending so much time in foster homes, ranging from the good and the bad to the ugly, and being shuffled around -sometimes in ways that felt absolutely random - from one new place to another, not knowing where I would end up, all of these things established unique cross-currents in my psyche. It taught me to be highly vigilant to social cues - the facial expressions of authority figures, the hopeful signs which signal a new person in my life could be a warm potential friend, or perhaps a cynical but channing user and abuser.

Living like this can be devastating for anyone, but exponentially more so for a child forced to adapt to constantly changing vistas and family power structures. Add the weight of the abuse suffered, and being molested by people I believed I could tust, and you must realize that for me and uncounted other kids life can be even more hurtful than you may have imagined.

My friend Billy, for example, was worse off than most of the other kids in our grade school, and certainly life had him more on the ropes than I was. We hung around a fairly substantial amount of the time, almost as if we were little veteran soldiers trying to heal up from the theatre of war that formed our common ex perience.

Billy always seemed nervous and upset, as if anticipating things he may have been unable to imagine. The smallest thing would set him off! After I had gotten into junior high, a friend and classmate asked me if I had heard about Billy. My reaction was to say "No, not a thing. What?" That's when I learned that my anxiety-stricken grade school chum had found a pistol among his dad's things. And that that pistol somehow went off while pointing at Dilly's young head. He was gone, and although no one said so out loud, it was fear-inducing and yet easy to imagine that Billy had suffered no accident but rather had self-terminated an existence that had simply become unbearable.

Shocked is not the word for how hearing that news and that imagining that darkest possibility had made me. My very closest friend took his own life. He had always ·seemed to be a wreck, and had never spoken a word about his life at home! It must have been far worse than anyone could imagine. He must have suffered beatings, or perhaps sadistic psychological abuse, and very likely a deadly combination. He and I had become friends because he and I were both quirky, and had an adventurous side that impelled us to explore almost all the terrain our small feet could allow us to traverse, but something down inside said to me, at the moment of learning Billy was no more, "He and I are more alike than what I had thought."

Maybe I was just lucky. Like Billy I was able to stuff my feelings deep down, but they didn't stay buried because there was always music to serve as my outlet! So those feelings found their way out disguised in melodies and exuberant passages of sound - either that I took in from the radio, the TV, or wherever I found them, or that I sung out into the world as my contribution to the rhythms and emotions of life itself.

The mirror doesn't lie, even though I can hide the sort of thought I want to conceal, or at least so I believe. Do I really have a poker face? Can others see and palpably sense the emotional pain that mostly Roger Thompson caused, through the ongoing sexual abuse he visited upon me, him being a full-grown man of 29 and me only a boy of seven. That was a devastating passage of experience! And it's hard to comprehend the burden of such things happening when a boy or a girl is that young, trying to put all these confusing and damaging incidents together and fitting them into the mental map of life and the world they're trying to assemble in their formative years.

First, I blamed myself for all the things that happened. I can never be sure why. May be it made more sense to my young mind than it did to believe that an adult on whom I depended for food and shelter would do anything heinous to me.

I came back to the Quad Cities - which used to encompass four cities but is now comprised of five, including Davenport and Bettendorf in southeastern Iowa, and Rock Island, Moline, and East Moline in northwestern Illinois - because of m y mother's passing. And the sex-capades in my life seem to stem from the abuse that filled my world as a child. Sometimes they have felt like a train out of control.

Vancouver was my first encounter with the troika of sex, drugs, and rock-and-roll! And I not only felt the hunger and the drive, but also the magnificently powerful force within not wanting to stop. Still, I knew I had to step away from the desire-spraking trio of influences or it would destroy me, as well as what unspoiled looks I had. You hear the stories of drug-abusers' teeth falling out between the age of 30 to 50 years. I just couldn't do it. I need to make a way out for myself, and I needed to do it quickly. Before, I couldn't stop. Just like my Troy-boy. He also admitted that he needed to stop, but he found that he couldn't. I kept telling myself that I wholeheartedly wanted not to go down that trail, and heard myself repetitiouslly saying "I will quit tomorrow!" But for many drug users tomorrow never comes, so they say!

Port Byron, Illinois is a small town, a Mississippi River hamlet, a beautiful meeting of riverbank and nowing water, both clements suggesting a pleasant eternity that awaits. On days off. I find that I can feel an indescribably smooth sense of contentment just to sit outside and enjoy watching the boats, barges, and people water skiing on the usually-mild river - which on stormy days is amazingly rough.

I had just moved to Port Byron when the Covid-19 pandemic hit. That was all I heard about on the news,. People were losing their jobs and companies that had been in the community for cons were cloing. It made me remember the terrible advent AIDS, and how it hit everywhere with a punch. I remember when the cause was still unknown, and how people referred to it for a time as "the gay cancer." People were feeling devastated, getting tired from their job over something nobody knew nothing of. Straight people were afraid to enter swimming pool ·at vacation resorts. Diners in fancy restaurants were afraid that their salads might be full of contaminants because a gay waiter had handled the plates.

So now if I get the sniffles and a fever, my job will not let me come back to work unless I undergo a lengthy quarantine, thinking it's the Covid-19. Today is May 6. 2020. Nothing is open at this time so I'm pulling that information in my book, my diary! Here it comes: the first wave of not knowing.

Don't worry, though. I never go to town and I know it'!. not Covid-19, but just a cold. I've been taking my sweatshirt on and off to regulate my body heat and comfort. I live out in the country and only make a quick stop for gas and/or food and then I take myself home! I live with a friend whom I've known for years! We hung around in the same social circle a few years ago. I knew his partner (roommate) for all you straight, wink wink and they knew mine. Gordon Muller, the financial adviser to the Democratic Party. It was fun back then!

Anyway. my roommate's partner passed away three years ago. Old age catches up to us all, unless, a tragedy arrive sooner. With things in disarray, it's hard going out anywhere. And you need to be selective on who comes through the door, even if it is the guy that ftXes your plumbing. I had an alterna tive: Sex and a lovely home or, 3!, my new roomma te aid," l'he homeless shelter has a room!"

Having been down that road, I don't need extra time to rca lite that if forced to choose between a homeless shelter or a $381,000 home, l'llta kc the home. Beside!> it's given me more to write about a nd to share. ·n,c life of a n artist, whatever kind of artist a person may be, is a crary life at some p(.·opl e l ive. Not a ll, but a select few! Well I did want a morc-than-U!,Uallifc and somehow I keep on finding it as the weeks. months and years tick away. Or docs it lind me? Either way, beautiful home a nd I do pay m y way with yardwork and other duties. llomcless shelter or here? That choice is simpl e. Meanwhile, it's not like I'm in tJ1e basement tied or chained up! I can live with it and cope with my new surroundings. My urroundings arc awesome. I'm up on a hill, writing my book while overlooking the Missi ssippi Ri ver on a sunny day. with nice brec7e to seal the deal.

FAITH, TRUST, INSIDE LEAD!

Aller moving back, I ·aw on the internet. America' Got I alen t- searching for that next big tar!'urc can I ing good enough. that i!, the quction? Do I have what i t takes? My oldest brother CB thinks I do, h is commen t: "You've got this," he th inks just because I have sung on two Gospel Television Shows. Jim Bakker fclcvision Show-refer to m y first book: Tantaliting Quest 04240, that on 5/3/20 a guy was going to purchase a book and wanted me to autograph. or sign it, I said sure. One more happy customer. It feels st ra nge to sign a book. I'm just a regular person, nothing special. At my age, to except flaws a nd all. Ju!.t because you know someone in the industry doesn't mean you have it made in the shade. Singing I what

I WB!, meant to do- Youtubc.com "The Most Wonderful I imc of the Year". recorded in the studio. and "It was" fun! And "I'll be hom e for Christmas". another studio with that jan flare. Li ve is a lot of fun. but nerve-racking, crowds and stagc fright. yup I have it! What really help is when I focus on things i n the back of the bui lding. 9.000 people wa the largest crowd in Moline. IL at a hockey game. I he national anthem. the have the la rgct scrccns and with no musi c, i t could be scary. Dean IJonowctt and good friend who cuts the hair for. Ryan'cacrcst and. imon Cowell, one of the judges for: America's Got Talent! till waiting for that last ca ll, who knows. what the outcome will be. You need to know, this is a talent show, not a singing show! I could lose to someone that can swallow knives or balance a spoon on the tip of their tongue. I ley. it could happen. you never know. Even though I ha ve duet with some of the biggest names i n the business, there arc no guara ntees in this t y pe of career. And there arc more down!. tha t include the Covid-19. talk about a sober ex perience, Debbie!)owner! But tJ1is is l ive get over it! Life is full of little disa ppoin tments. You just need to keep you r head up, and look for tha t open door, pot at the end of the rainbow. ott hat stu IT tha t you smoke, not included. Following your heart and you r dream, two of the ha rdetthings ever. More people tum to their fai th in times oftroublc. "Oh God please help me" I tJlink that's how it gocl. And then afler he helps them, they forget abou t him and what they B!,kcd for. I've seen a nd met more people that don't even have a religimLfaith based that arc more kind and cari ng. You've heard the phrase "so heavenl y bound, no earth l y good", I'm sure you know where I am going with th is! My father's ide are Cathol ic and J ewish. so my cousins arc a tive American J ews, what a combo... I'm not about to a k I lashem for anything, I will strive for it. and if I get it, or achieve it, fine, if not, then I wi ll just move on and sec what the next chapter holds for me.

John Collings, who lived in the Quad-Cities for 10 years, said using his voice got him into the entertainment industry, numerous people from friends to co-workers to even celebrities that he met - told John Collings that he ought to write a book. So he did.

ILLINOIS SENIORS ON MEDICARE ARE GETTING A BIG PAY DAY

"Tantalizing Quest 04240" tells the former Quad-City performer's story, from his first big break going to work for the Burt Reynolds Dinner Theatre in Jupiter, Fla., to the Quad-City connections that led him to sing with the Nelson Riddle Orchestra, to auditioning for Ryan Seacrest's short-lived talk show to an ill fated stint on televangelist Jim Bakker's comeback TV show. "I wanted to move on. I put everything into writing it," said Collings, who now lives in Burlington, Iowa. "It seemed like several chapters had passed by, and it was the right time to do it and go from there." Collings tells of his tumultuous childhood, raised by a Native American father and Irish mother, then going to a series of foster homes. By age 17, he was on his own. But he knew he could sing. Even at age 9, he said, he would wander the playground singing and drew a crowd of children following him. "I knew at that point that I was going to use my voice," he said. He lived in the Quad-Cities, in the Gold Coast neighborhood, from 1992 to 2002, and sang with the Quad-City Kix Orchestra. Linda Little, wife of orchestra director Steve Little, introduced him to orchestra leader Nelson Riddle's son Skipper, and Collings got to sing with the orchestra in 1998.

Collings went to Los Angeles to meet up with friend Dean Banowetz - the DeWitt, Iowa, native who went on to Hollywood to become hairdresser for "American Idol" - won a singing contest there, and auditioned to be the "courtyard correspondent" on "Idol" host Ryan Seacrest's short-lived talk show.

From there, he went to Branson, Mo., and became a backup singer and makeup artist on Bakker's daily talk show. He left after claiming the host made advances toward him.

The book is available online, through Barnes & Noble's Website, www.bn.com.

"It touches about everything that someone can relate to," he said. "But there were some triumphs that happen in the book as well."

TANTALIZING QUEST

by John Collings

What's Jim Bakker doing in Branson, Missouri– that mecca of family -oriented entertainment, country-western theater and whole some, all-American young people striving for the big time?And how did a nice Midwestern boy with a great singing voice wind up on Jim Bakker's newest television show - only to be groped by the minister himself, then harassed by his minions, and finally tossed off the show entirely?

The answers are in Tantalizing Quer 04 40, a factual recounting that rips away the secrecy and exposes the curious world of televangelism. This searing insider's account turns the hot lights on the P.T. Barnum of evangelicals– Jim Bakker himself.

Tantalizing Quer 04..140 is John Collings's ca utionary and true story of just how difficult the climb to stardom can be.

John Collings

My first audition was in Las Vegas, NV January 7, 2020 at the Rio Casino. It wasn't as crowded as I thought but after Gabrielle Union got done slamming the show, what could you expect! And complaining about Simon Cowell smoking in his office. "Really?" The whole thing she said was race about blacks. How in the hell, does that have to do with Simon Cowell smoking in his offtce? I really thought she liked the show and they liked her, but afler she started all that crap, I wouldn't renew her contract either. You really never hear about our people Native Americans start an uproar unless you put a pipeline through our burial cemetery plots in the Dakota's. I was upset about that and felt the government could have put it another place!

May 28-29 is when America's Got Talent will start airing. I could get a call between now and a week beforehand. Always check my emails, that gets old after a while. I will be glad when a week before arrives, then get the verdict, "yes" or "no", it's the not knowing. Hopefully after the Covid-19 is over things will get back to normal, and I can get back to singing with the orchestra. Big band music has always been my thing, and can sing pop, country, light rock-like Joumcy, REO- pecdwagon, Gospel etc.

Like everyone, I'm just trying to hang on and get through this ordeal in a crazy world! Although things seem shaky, we all need to live the life that we are given, and I hope make improvements for our wellbeing.

BRANSON MO FAME CONNECTION

Even though this small town, you wouldn't think it holds such star power! Nashville, a big city the place where I met Roy Callaway, works closely with country star Garth Brook -and said: Thomas if you could only sing country, I could make you a star!

Branson, a place where you could pull up to a stoplight look next to you and see Jimmy Osmond in a very small car! You'd never know it but Branson is a very clickish town and getting a singing job is difficult. You almost need to know someone like I did. Duets with Bucky heard, and our band was Tony Orlands Band. Because the whole band went to church there, the band was awesome. Bucky Heard ended up auditioning for Bill Medley, of Righteous Brother Fame. After he was a Righteous Brother for so long, Bucky changed. His head apparently got larger and he became too good. I was no longer in his league! Although at singing what he was now asked to ing my voice was ideal.

Youtube.com "Most Wonderful Time of the Year" John Collings.

Bucky was a rock singer and his voice was groomed for that style. I had defended him on many occasions, a fact that he knew about. Righteous Brother die-hard fans wanted nothing to do with Bucky and they were more than happy to let him know. That's where I came in, I had noticed at the very bottom of some of the videos the displeasure int eh comments and tried to sway some of the fans, that this new singer could never take on Billie Hatfield's place but need to be there. "The show must go on" as they say, and Mill Medley needs Bucky for just that. The sad part, I really thought because, Buck Heard claims to be "born again" this could never happen, the rejection! Our friendship down the toilet and him snubbing me... One thing I learned from the Osmond, it's a job, that's all and be yourself! Partied with Andy, song writer for Lady Gaga! John Wayne Jr. illegitimate son, we met in Florida, he was flying back and forth from Punta Gorda to him, stayed for a moth then left!

Jaime Jo Reynolds, But's niece was a lot of fun, drove to Hollywood, Florida- discos were big and she wanted to dance. 1980's we saw each other a lot because I worked at the ranch. Burt Reynold Ranch in Jupiter Florida. First heard about it on a Barbra Walters special. Packed my stuff went with two bags and I was gone, not recommended no adays. I was young and wanted to see the lifestyle, single and board!

Roy Callaway- who works with country singer Garth Brooks, wanted to make me a star, only I can't sing country music! Darn! Viril Osmond wanted to record me and produce me, but they all want money upfront! I have to admit, my life has been interesting and we all have interesting lives! My foster mother picked cotton in Arkansas, and told me how her hands would bleed. Now of course there are machines that do all the work. People today would bever and could not imagine ever working a job like that. Young people today could never imagine, working that hard. But when work is scarce. you do what you need to survive. These are things. I feel not only are important, but educational. Don't you? I've lived both spectrums of life, some good and some painful to talk about. Isn't that what make life interesting and in some way molds us to be whom we become in life. And yes, I could have said poor me, on some of the happenings but why? It doesn't change things. However, it's how we choose to handle it as we grow! No matter how old you are never stop the learning process, it can make you a better person. Even working around celebs learn form them, take the good part and if you can apply it, do so...

Life is like the ripples on water! Here for a short time, use time as wisely as possible. We are all just people, people who need people! Covid-19 has changed my plans, like my audition for America's Got Talent, a TV show made for talent and not just singers! But also this gave me time to reflect on my life, and keep you posted on from April 2006 up until now! And parting with Andi, a writer for Lady Gaga my most recent of star entanglement, it was fun though, and hot to get together again for more of that awesome fantastic memorable fun!

AGAINST THE GRAIN

Trump, not everyone's favorite, as pointed out by this, about in her 80's Lady, how people that aren't wearing masks must be Trump supporters! I hear about it on a daily basis and here I am with a mask on.

I love people like that, I can learn from her, believe me. Some thoughts should be left in your head and not shared with people around you. Especially in line at the check out counter, with a long line behind you that probably doesn't care, and do not give a _____ about your views on the subject! llopcfully I can write about this and not get pissed off! All my thoughs about what she was saying I kept in my head and that was very difficult. A lot of people just jump on the bandwagon because other people are doing it as well, or just want to be heard because nobody is listening at home! People, not all, but some never fact find, just blurt out crap because others are and have not basis!

Donald Trump's job is not easy, and if he knew now back then, that he would get treated like this, maybe he would change his mind. The ones who took on that career change have not all been good at it. My partner was the financial adviser to the Democratic Party, "Gordon Muller", wrote the checks for the Democratic Party in Davenport, Iowa! Gordon, a full-blood German, and a math teacher for the Pleasant Valley school system in Davenport, Iowa. When candidates were in town, we had the opportunity to meet and greet. Things were a lot different back then! Not all this critical stuff, like Pelosi- ripping up president Trumps speech, and I know she thought it was clever but she in turn made the democrats look bad and her insinuation of Trump being overweight- not good! We never had this back when I was a Democrat, and this is why I left the party .... Think about it, do you blame me? To think someone would do this on national television and think that was okay! I don't care who our leader is, show some respect and don't be stupid... What does that say to new Democrats, they are looking up to this party and looking for direction? Is this the path you want to bring them down, I hope not! Democrats were so respectful back when I was and never painted negative crap, it saddens me that it has come down to this... And will Democrats ever recover form thes sad events? Time will tell, Pete Buttigieg would have made me rethink and probably changed back. He's presidential material and has the looks of a Kennedy, star power and the party should have backed him, it's sad he didn't come through-

Wow, what the Democrats could have done with this guy, he just has what it takes to get the political party back on its feet. It's not because he's gay but because how he holds himself in the public's·eye. For heaven's sake. rethink this and bring him on board. He should have gotten that opportunity to make it happen! For one thing the Democrats are making it interesting, I can't wait to see what happens next! What ever happened to that olden day, disagreement, and then we moved on!

Madonna wants to bum down the white house and kill Donald Trump! The HATE is unbelievable, and gay churches have stickers on their doors, "No Hate Here", I guess it just is promoted and festers there but take it outside. For God's sake, for Pete's sake we don't want people to know if it's okay, to preach it from the pulpit, but not we are just exercising our right.

What happened to church and state being set apart? Some so-called pastors do not see the damage they are causing and are blind sighted... and now Trump wants churches to open to gather and everyone pray, as we should always! We all believe and in our darkest hour, more so don't you agree? That is the human part of us, and a lot of young are tired of staying at home, feeling cooped up. Remember this is a pandemic, and need to be under control first. Bible times, even the Jews get tired of eating mannah and wanted meat! God granted their desires and heard their plead of discontent. Nothing new, only this is worse, and yes, our lives are turned upside-down, but if we stick to social distancing and always have on our masks, "except in bed", we will come out of this on top!

In the scriptures it does talk about a change in population, the amount of non-Jews and Jews on the earth. Could this be that element that changes.

Hope that we don't have any more testing to escape any labs. See none of us are perfect, no matter how we perceive ourselves! And all the gadgets will not make us better than the next, yes Bucky Heard I am referring this to you. Death is inevitable and when our time is up, just ask Ben Stiller, his father just passed away. RIP, sir and thank you for the laughter that you gave us through the years! Jew, gentile, Greek, it's going to happen. unless you are Enock, but he will be back to earth and die and return to Hashem (G-d). See some are faithful and really seek the love of the Great One!!!

AUTHOR BIOGRAPHY

John Collings wrote his remarkable book **Tantalizing Quest 04240** in 2006. It opened wide a light of saturated window onto televangelism, the shady underbelly of the entertainment world, and was an unpredictable jaunt down many of the diverse paths this peripatetic singing artist has pursued with his particular flair and vision.

Like its 2006 predecessor, **America Has Talent/Against the Grain**, the 2020 book now in your hands. goes deep into the absurdly comical-yet-disturbing world of televangelical confidence games. It rips open the hypocrisy of such "giants" of the field as Jim Bakker, the disgraced (though back for another payday) "minister" who originally set the stage for

Tammy Faye Bakker's stardom an enterprise that backfired on him eventually -and who isn't averse to backstage-groping a boy or two as he tries with a new broadcast partner to recapture the lightning of those days when melting mascara and hankie-wringing lured viewers to send in those donation they likely couldn't really afford.

Collings, a gifted singer and performer, has been deep inside the belly of the beast and has emerged to share a dish fashioned from the innards. That's just the appetizer for a book that takes a unique look at numerous other aspects of life in this intense and unpredictable moment in time.

The author currently lives in in the riverside city of Port Byron. Illinois. He is one-quarter Passamaquoddy, an American Indian people whose traditional domain spans northeastern North America and Canada. Collings is the grandson of a Royal Canadian Mountie, father to two grown children and grandfather to five youngsters.

Printed in the United States
By Bookmasters